TSUBU the Little Snail

by Carol Ann Williams illustrated by Tatsuro Kiuchi

SIMON & SCHUSTER BOOKS FOR YOUNG READERS

SIMON & SCHUSTER BOOKS FOR YOUNG READERS
An imprint of Simon & Schuster Children's Publishing Division, 1230 Avenue of the Americas, New York, New York 10020. Book design by Lucille Chomowicz. The text for this book is set in 16-point Cloister. The illustrations were done in oils. Manufactured in the United States of America. 10 9 8 7 6 5 4 3 2 1

Library of Congress Cataloging-in-Publication Data: Williams, Carol Ann. Tsubu the little snail / by Carol Ann Williams ; illustrated by Tatsuro Kiuchi. p. cm. Summary: When an elderly couple pray for a son, the Water God sends them a snail boy who grows up to marry a noble's daughter. [1. Folklore—Japan.] I. Kiuchi, Tatsuro, ill. II. Title.
PZ8.1.W649Ts 1995 398.2—dc20 [E] 93-49344 CIP AC ISBN: 0-671-87167-6

To my friend Miki—T. K.

For Pietro,
with thanks to Bebe—C. A. W.

Once, a long, long time ago, there lived a rice farmer and his wife. They worked in the rice paddies of the *choja*, a rich and powerful landowner. They were so poor they sometimes had nothing to eat. Even so, what they wanted most in the world was not riches or food, but a baby.

The years went by and no baby came to them.

One day, as the wife was working, she prayed out loud to the Water God. "Please hear me, Honorable Water God. Please give us a baby, any baby at all, even a frog or a little snail like the ones here in this rice paddy. We will love him and care for him no matter who he is."

That night the rice farmer and his wife were blessed with the baby they had dreamed of for so long.

He was a little snail. And though he was not a boy, he was theirs and they were happy. They named him *Tsubu,* "little snail." To honor the Water God who had sent him, they put Tsubu in a bowl of water in front of their household shrine. They loved him and cared for him and fed him as they would any growing boy.

Twenty years passed. Tsubu did not grow. Tsubu's father was now an old farmer and his work was harder than ever. He groaned as he loaded his three horses with the yearly rice tax he had to pay to the powerful choja.

Suddenly, he heard a loud voice coming from inside the house. "Father, Father! Let me help!"

"What is this?" mumbled the old farmer as he hurried inside.

"I'll deliver the rice for you, Father," said Tsubu.

The old man stared in amazement at his son, who had never spoken before. He called to his wife to come and see this miracle.

"You have taken such good care of me," said Tsubu. "Now it is time for me to go out into the world. Today *I* will take the rice tax to the choja."

"But how will you do that?" asked his mother.

"How will you drive the horses?" asked his father.

"You'll see," said Tsubu. "Just put me up on one of the rice bales."

The old farmer did not think this sounded like a good idea at all. There was no way his son could drive the horses, and since Tsubu was so little there was a good chance he'd get hurt. But he was a gift from the Water God. So the farmer gently lifted Tsubu out of the water bowl and carefully placed him on the highest bale of rice.

"Don't worry, Mother and Father. I'll be back soon," Tsubu happily told them. With that he called out to the horses, "*Haido, haido shishi,* giddy-up, giddy-up," and drove out the gate and down the road.

Tsubu drove the team like an expert horseman. Through streams and over bridges they went. All the while he sang the songs that the drivers sing. His voice was so clear and strong that the horses trotted along in time to the music. The bells on their necks rang in tune, *janka gonka,* jingle jangle. It was glorious!

The people working in the rice fields heard the singing and looked up. The people walking along the road heard the singing and looked up. All the people stared in amazement. Here were the old farmer's three horses. And there were the rice bales. But where was the driver? They thought it was very strange.

The servants at the choja's house also thought it was very strange. They too stared in amazement. They saw the farmer's three horses trot in the gate all alone. But they heard a loud voice commanding, "*Hai, hai, shan shan,* whoa!"

"Where is the driver?" one asked.

"These horses couldn't have come by themselves," said another.

"This is very strange," said a third.

From his perch amidst the bales of rice Tsubu hollered, "Not strange at all, my friends! I have brought the yearly rice tax. Please help me down."

"What? Who is that?" the servants exclaimed.

"It is *I,*" said Tsubu.

The servants searched in the rice bales until they found him.

"Why, he's just a snail," said the servant who was holding the farmer's son gingerly in his palm.

Tsubu looked up at the big man. "I'm sorry I'm so small. If you would unload the rice for me, I would be very grateful. Just put me on the edge of the porch and, please, be careful not to crush me."

The servants were very surprised to hear a snail talking. They put him down and quickly called for the master. "A snail! Master! A snail has brought the rice tax!"

Hearing the commotion, the grand choja came out onto the porch. Sure enough, there was Tsubu, and there were the three horses and the yearly rice tax piled high behind them. Soon others from the household came out to see. They stared in amazement.

The choja had heard that the Water God had given one of the farmers a snail for a son, but he had never imagined that this snail could talk and drive horses just like a real person. He bent down to the little snail. "Are you really the farmer's son?" he asked.

"I am," replied the snail in a loud voice. "I am twenty years old, and I am helping my father."

The choja was very impressed. He ordered his servants to unload the bales of rice and to feed the three horses. Then he invited the little snail into the house for dinner. He set him down on the edge of a large tray.

The first course was rice. Though no one could tell how it happened, all of Tsubu's rice disappeared. The second course was soup. Slowly, little by little, the soup disappeared. The third course was fish. In the same mysterious way, it too disappeared. The little snail had eaten as much as any grown man! And like a grown man, he politely thanked his host for the delicious meal.

"Snail Boy," said the choja, "you are so special, I would like you to be my son-in-law."

Tsubu could not believe his ears. "Do you mean it?" he asked.

"Yes," said the choja. "You may have one of my daughters as your wife." And he called for his two daughters.

"Which of you wants to marry the Snail Boy?" he asked.

The older daughter wrinkled up her nose. "Ugh!" she snapped. "Marry a slimy snail? That's disgusting!" She stomped out of the room.

The younger daughter, however, was gentle and kind. "Do not worry," she told her father. "If you promised that one of us would marry the little snail, I will go."

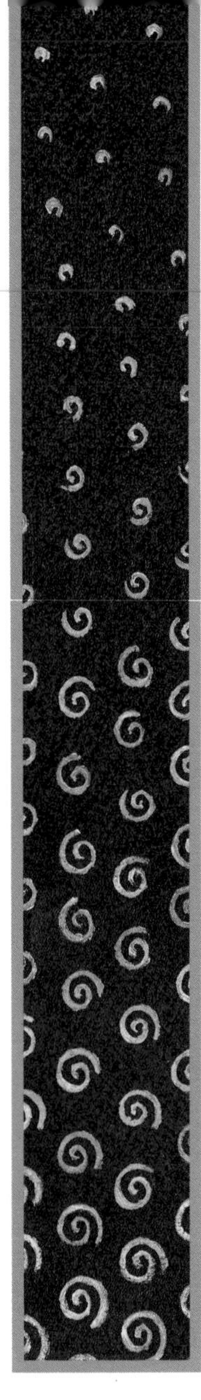

So it came to pass that the choja's younger daughter married Tsubu.

She came with a dowry of seven chests of goods and seven trunks of kimonos and seven times seven suitcases. She came with so much that not even seven horses could carry it all. And since there was no room for it in the farmer's little cottage, the choja built a large storehouse for all of his daughter's belongings.

The fact that she could not use these things did not bother the choja's daughter one bit. The bride was glad to be living in the farmer's cottage with her new husband, for she loved him, even though he was a snail.

She quickly became a part of the family.

She worked hard in the rice fields during the day, and in the evening helped with the household chores. The little snail's old parents had never been more comfortable. And Tsubu had never been happier. His wife chatted and laughed with him as she moved about the cottage. Sometimes she even sat by his water bowl, without speaking, just to be near him.

And so the time passed.

Spring came and with it came the festival of the God of Healing. Tsubu's wife wanted to join in the celebrations.

"I'd like to go with you," said Tsubu.

This made his wife very happy. She powdered her face. She fixed her hair. She put on the prettiest kimono in all of her seven trunks. She looked as beautiful as a flower.

She placed Tsubu in the front fastener of her sash. Together they set off to the festival. Along the way they talked and laughed just as they did at home. People heard their merry conversation but saw no one except the beautiful girl.

"Why, she's talking to herself," they said, shaking their heads. "What a shame she's gone crazy."

She didn't care what they said. She kept on chatting with her husband until they came to the shrine of the God of Healing. She decided to go in and pray.

Tsubu wanted to stay outside. "It's such a nice spring day," he said. "I'd like to rest out here. Put me by the side of the road and I will wait for you."

"All right," she agreed, "if that is what you want. But be careful. Don't let a bird swoop down and eat you up."

"I'll be fine," said Tsubu, who was already basking in the warm sun.

Tsubu's wife carefully put him at the edge of the path where no one would step on him. "I'll say one prayer and be right back," she told him. She hurried up the hill to the temple. As she had promised, she said one prayer, then hurried back to her husband.

But he was not where she had left him. She searched along the path. Where was he? She called, "Tsubu? Tsubu, where are you?" There was no answer.

Not wanting to think that a bird had eaten him, she decided that he must have fallen into the rice paddy. She searched along the edge. He was not there. She stepped into the muddy water, searching. She waded out into the center of the rice fields, picking up every snail she saw.

She did not stop all through the long day. Her beautiful kimono grew wet and dirty. Her face was splattered with mud. She sang a mournful song to the husband she had lost.

People walking home from the festival heard her song and looked up. They shook their heads. "Such a beautiful girl. What a shame she's gone crazy."

And still she searched. Desperately, she dropped to her knees in the mud. As she landed she heard a cracking sound beneath her. She reached into the mud and pulled out a broken shell. "Oh, Water God," she cried, "I think I have killed my husband! Oh, I cannot go on! I would rather drown myself than live without him!"

But as she started to throw herself into the water, a loud voice rang out, "Stop! Don't do that!"

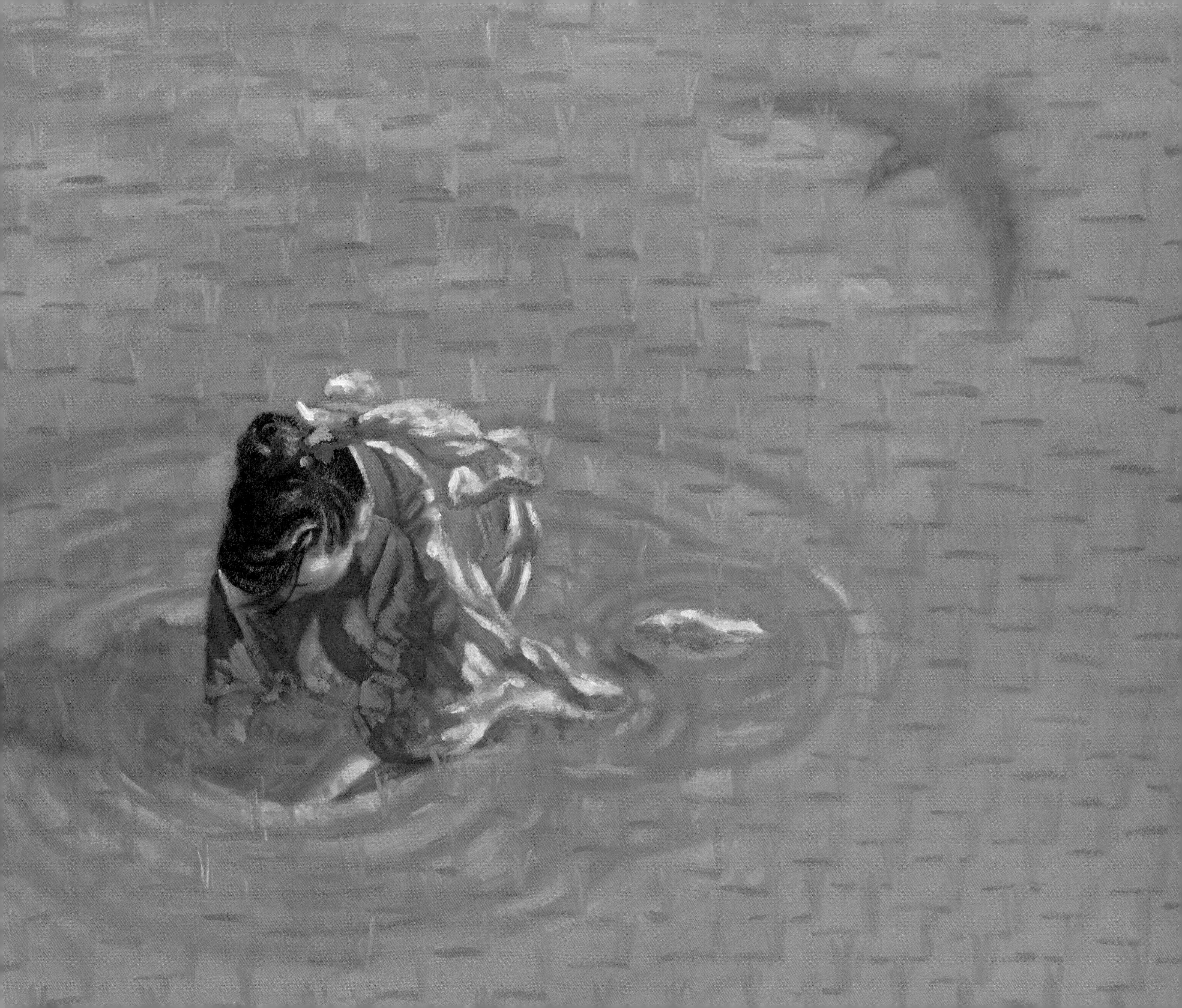

She turned to see a handsome young man standing behind her.

"I am the child of the Water God," he said. "I have been disguised as a little snail. But today, because you searched for me without caring what other people thought, my shell broke and I became a real person." He took her hands in his. "Because you loved me, I am now your real husband."

She was overjoyed.

And so were the old farmer and his wife.

And so was the choja, who held a banquet in their honor.

The choja then built the happy couple a mansion. There they prospered. They built Tsubu's parents a lovely home and took care of their every need. The old farmer and his wife were never hungry again. All their struggles were over.

And their precious son, once a little snail, was known far and wide as the grand Snail Choja.

Author's Note

Over the centuries, this classic Japanese folktale has been told countless times. The details vary in the many tellings, but the message always stays the same: Life is sacred. No matter how insignificant it may seem, it is to be loved and respected. It is also a source of joy.

The origins of the story lie in Shintoism, the ancient native religion of Japan, with its emphasis on recognizing the fundamental mystery at the heart of all things. This mystery was embodied in the *kami,* or gods. The fact that the snail in this folktale is the son of the Water God—the kami of the rice fields—signifies that his essence is divine. Those who love him honor this essence. In so doing, they affirm the sacred in all of us.

I read several versions of this tale. My sources included *Folktales of Japan*, edited by Keigo Seki and translated by Robert J. Adams, University of Chicago Press, 1963. The tales in that book came from Seki's *Mukashi-banashi* (Japanese Folktales), a three-volume collection of 240 folktales published in 1956–57. Keigo Seki was one of the foremost early scholars to collect, publish, and classify Japanese folktales. I also drew knowledge from a contemporary Japanese retelling, "The Snail Choja," by Teiji Seda, a selection in the anthology *Ancient Japanese Tales*, published by Gakken Publishing Co., Tokyo, n.d. This retelling was orally translated for me by my friend Junko Edahiro, who is an editor at Sunmark Publishing Co., Tokyo. It was by Junko's grace that I came to a true understanding of the spiritual heart of the story.